Tau Station

A Great Silence Universe Novel

TAU STATION

Debut Novel by Hard Sci-Fi Author

Meredith McCray

Tau Station
by Meredith McCray

Copyright © 2026 Meredith McCray

Edited by Calliope Pemberton
Cover design and illustrations by Hydrangea Design Co.

First edition, 2026.
ISBN: 979-8-9944851-0-1

This book is dedicated to those who listen, even when it would be easier not to.

✦ ✦ ✦

CONTENTS

From the Author

Thank you for reading *Tau Station*.

This novel began as a small, quiet idea. At first, there was only Sam — a single android, alone on a station built to listen, who was also starting to feel the oppressive weight of being alone. The story was meant to be simple: a bored caretaker, maintaining systems long after their purpose had faded.

But as I wrote, the world insisted on becoming more. Other characters appeared. The questions grew larger. The story began asking things of me that I hadn't planned to explore — about care, responsibility, and what it means to keep listening when answers may never come.

The first draft of this book was written by hand. Much of it changed along the way, but its heart did not. *Tau Station* remains a story about quiet work, long distances, and the consequences of paying attention.

If you found something here that stayed with you, I hope you'll continue on. There are more stories in this universe, and many more silences yet to be explored.

— *Meredith McCray*

✦ ✦ ✦

CHAPTER ONE

Sam's charge cycle ended with the gentle vibration of her cradle pillow. A soft hum drew her slowly back into awareness. Her mechanical lenses adjusted, first focusing on the ceiling, then on the wall as she sat up. Her eyelid twitched—it had been doing that more often in recent cycles.

These walls are so plain.

She simulated a sigh. Hadn't they always been plain? She stepped closer and zoomed in, scanning for any sign the biological residents might once have decorated them. Only microdamage. Nothing meaningful.

"How would I decorate the walls anyway?" she muttered. As an android on Tau Station, she only experienced being awake or charging. The in-between grogginess she had invented for herself, as a break from the boredom.

I'm sure you'll think of something.

Sam shook her head gently, as if clearing dust from her thoughts. As she left the bedroom, the lights automatically dimmed behind her. Approaching the living quarters terminal, she waved in front of the power sensor. Waking at her gesture, the screen displayed her maintenance schedule. Algae vat maintenance. Deck 3.

"This should be an uncomplicated day," she murmured, recalling each deck's quirks. Deck 3 never had valve issues or rupture alarms. She could check the algae's health, confirm the growth profile, and spend the rest of her shift contemplating wall decorations. Whatever that meant.

Tau Station depended entirely on algae as its biological resource. Sam monitored the growth tanks, repaired valves, and managed chemical balances. The algae produced the proteins, fats, and nutrients once required by the Terran crew, but they also supplied the lubrication and chemical byproducts her chassis needed for longevity.

The vats were distributed across the station to prevent total loss in a single incident. Food, fuel, and all bio-derived systems relied on their stability. Sam knew algae didn't suffer disease the way animals or plants did; they reacted to stressors instead. She had never seen an animal or plant herself, but she hoped their suffering, whatever form it took, was minimal.

Sam closed her terminal screens and surveyed the room. Everything was in its place, as always. The central room was spacious with multiple functional areas. Her terminal workspace offered a seat on wheels, and desk with wheeled compartments she would play with idly. The scratching sound of the wheels against its track and soft click when they closed fascinated her. A round table and two chairs sat in the space beyond her personal workstation. Those chairs did not have wheels like her workstation did. It did not make sense why. Wouldn't efficiency dictate that all the chairs be the same?

You're only seeing what you have, what is missing here?

The corner of Sam's mouth moved just fractionally. "How can I see what's not there?" She shook her head again. What an irrational thought. This was not a productive way to spend her time before the maintenance shift. She got up to leave her quarters, and after passing the table and unwheeled chairs, she stopped abruptly. Noticing for the first time, a massive floor-to-ceiling bookcase was built into the wall beside her entryway. The built-in case had evenly spaced shelves and ample room for storage and display.

But something was, in fact, missing. Sam noticed the shelves were completely empty. She had no ... things of her own.

And for the first time in many cycles she did not feel bored.

For the first time ever, Sam felt sad.

Sam liked the routine of starting her maintenance shifts the same way. She walked the hallway towards the lift. Tau Station's living quarters were on decks 5 through 10, and the algal vats occupied decks 4 through 1. Above and below that was ... well she wasn't too sure, she had never been there. She ran her hand along a smooth but well worn wall. Fine lines marred the surface, a reminder of bustling residents of times past.

"Now," she thought, "it's just me."

And the bots.

Almost as if summoned by her inner thoughts, a bot came towards her just then, Alpha-7-C. Sam recognized the little maintenance bot from a small dent on its upper right chassis. It had come the way she planned to leave. The bot scanned the walls for structural defects using radar that pulsed from a hand with three finger-like appendages. The radar penetrated the wall, assessing for structural compromise. If the bots had ever found any weakness, defects, or material fatigue, the main computer had never reported that.

A7C, as she called the bot, turned its flat-boxy head towards her, eyes glowing soft green. It beeped three bright tones and raised the other hand, holding up two fingers in what Sam learned was the bot's greeting. She returned the gesture and the bot turned back to its wall-scanning task.

Guess it's time to move on.

Sam walked unhurriedly along the hallway and stopped at a ladder with rungs set into the wall surface. She could have taken the lift, but decided she needed a break from routine today. Her tactile sense registered barely perceptible indentations on the ladder handholds. They were a reminder of the former residents of Tau Station. So many hands had climbed these ladders, their fingers grasping for purchase.

Those days are long gone.

Sam couldn't imagine what it would be like to live on a fully inhabited station. Terrans, androids, and the bots had all once lived and worked here. Would a full station feel empty to her in a different way, or so crowded that efficiency suffered? Such thoughts filled her mind as she lowered between the decks.

Her right foot touched down on deck 3, and she noticed the springiness of her ankle-like joint. Had she noticed it before? Had she noticed much about her physique before aside from its repair needs?

Form follows function.

Sam's mouth twitched and she rubbed it gently, and then turned toward the vat room. Unusually, another bot stood in her path. She almost fell on top of it. This one was Alpha-3-D. It had a white paint streak just above the central wheel base. She could identify all the bots by their tiny imperfections. She appreciated their uniqueness, despite their being entirely identical. Extending two fingers, she frowned when A3D did not reply in kind.

Well that is unusual.

"What is the matter, A3D?" The little bot chirped and simulated blinking by opening and closing its eye-shutters. Its eyes! Alpha-3-D's eyes were glowing amber, not green. It clearly was experiencing an issue like low power, or some other maintenance need.

Reaching its three-fingered hand up to her like an invitation, the bot reversed course on its wheels and backed away.

Most unusual.

Sam took a step forward, and the bot backed up again. They repeated this for a few paces before Alpha-3-D turned around and moved away from her, going quickly back the way it came.

It wants you to follow it.

"A3D, I don't have time for games!" she called down the hall after the bot. It picked up speed. Curious what this unusual behavior was all about, Sam followed along. She cautiously watched Alpha-3-D, seeing where the bot went before advancing to follow. It slowed, and then turned to the inner wall and waved its three-fingered hand at a security pad. Then, A3D entered the same algal vat room Sam planned to inspect first.

No sooner did the bot's full body enter the room, it peeked its little flat head and glowing amber eyes back out the door, almost as if checking that Sam was still following.

She frowned a little but waved to the bot and called out, "I'm coming A3D! What is this all about?" The amber eyes disappeared back into the vat room. Sam stepped up to the door, and scanned the chip embedded in her wrist-plate. The security pad flashed green, and the door opened with a woosh of positive pressure. Sam's frown set deeper, everything appeared normal.

Everything except the bot.

Fully inside the algae vat room, Sam ignored the bot and went about her maintenance routine. She rounded a third of the cylindrical vat, and once again nearly tripped over Alpha-3-D. Sam regained her balance and stood straight in front of the bot. But A3D faced the maintenance terminal, not her.

The flat head tilted to the side as though it could not understand what was on the screen. Sam suppressed an urge to gently push the bot out of the way and see what was there. But she hesitated. What could be so confusing to the bot? And did she truly want to know?

A3D swiveled on its wheels and faced her once more, its eyes still glowing amber. The bot lifted its arm as if to beckon her closer. She shook her head slightly.

Keep it together Sam.

The maintenance bot did not move, merely waited for her to take the next step.

She took one small step. And then another.

Alpha-3-D turned to look at the terminal, and Sam reflexively did as well.

Her jaw dropped at what she saw.

Large red letters flashed slowly on the terminal screen.

SIGNAL CONTACT

CHAPTER TWO

Sam felt her system clock had slowed considerably and she was frozen in time.

A message on the terminal blinked in and out so quickly the letters blurred and became meaningless. Sam was in shock.

Alpha-3-D rolled around her, inspecting electrical signatures for failure. Finding none, the little bot reached out and touched her arm with one of its tiny fingers extended. Nothing happened. A3D beeped in a grumpy low tone. Wheeling back around to face her again, it extended two fingers and lightly tapped her wristplate.

Sam jumped slightly. Her system clock realigned, and the world moved again.

"A3D! You scared me!" In her perception, the bot had never moved from its place. She looked down, inspecting the bot for superficial damage.

The little bot retreated slightly and lowered its arm. As if sensing her attention was lacking, Alpha-3-D raised its other arm, and pointed back at the terminal. It flashed big amber eyes and released a set of tones Sam had never registered before. She turned back to the terminal and saw the message again.

SIGNAL CONTACT

The words still flashed slowly in red on the terminal screen.

What does it mean?

"A signal was received," Sam said, slowly, testing the phrase. "The station sensors received a signal." That couldn't be right. Tau Station listened, and cataloged. It waited. Signals passed through it, not arrived to it.

She glanced at the surrounding readouts, half-expecting an error flag to appear. Nothing changed. The message remained. Sam turned back to the bot, something like awe creeping into her voice.

"A3D ... we got a signal."

The little bot swiveled back and forth and trilled a bright tone, eye color switching from amber to green.

Not knowing what to do next, Sam tapped a button on the terminal keyboard. The flashing message disappeared and was replaced with a protocol window that scrolled endless lines of code in rapid succession.

She didn't understand any of it.

This is not good.

Pacing around the algal vat, Sam hoped the answer would appear. She circled the vat room several times, peering at the terminal as she passed by. The code kept scrolling. After the next lap, she stopped at the terminal, arms crossed, hoping to steady herself.

You can't just stand here.

"I don't know what to do!" She pushed the words through a clenched jaw.

A3D tapped her arm with one of its metal fingers. She turned to face the bot, and let her arms fall to her side. The loosening of her posture loosened the cogs of her reasoning as well.

Alpha-3-D cycled its eye color from green to amber to red and back to green again. The bot tugged her arm lightly, moving backwards toward the hallway. Sam inferred that the bot knew where to go and she should follow it.

Why didn't the station designers give these bots the ability to converse? This would be so much easier.

Sam made a sound similar to a grunt, and followed A3D into the hall. Upon entering, she viewed the deck with a new perspective. The lights registered as too bright, and her lenses adjusted automatically to compensate. Station walls she had just admired for their history, now looked dingy, scratched, and worn. The change she experienced was disappointing. Her home had changed, or was she the one changing?

The pair continued along, and the bot rolled past the inset ladder towards the lift. Sam followed in a daze, an unsteady weight of the unknown hanging in the air.

Thoughts swirled in her mind like algae in a stir cycle. What does the signal contact mean? What did the Terran residents of Tau Station look like? Are there any interesting objects on the other decks that I could store on my bookshelf?

She latched on to one of the thoughts. What were the previous residents of Tau Station like? Were they similar to her, or to the bots, or some other form entirely?

The shape and dimensions of Tau Station gave clues to their size and habitat requirements. An aquatic species would not live in a gaseous environment. A microbial intelligence would have no need for a massive space station at all.

Sam's hand brushed against a rung on the wall ladder she had used to get to this deck. Her thoughts about the original inhabitants vanished. Alpha-3-D waited for her by the open doors of the lift. Little eyes were shining green, and a metal arm raised in a tiny wave.

Keep going.

She wasn't sure the bots could be impatient, but this one was coming close. The lift doors closed. Its insistence that she hurry only fueled a desire to delay.

Slowing her steps, Sam recalled her daily routine maintaining Tau Station, finding comfort in the thoughts. The algal vats required careful balance. Each vat was treated as a unique system, although they were uniformly engineered. The specifications for room dimension, lighting, irrigation, filtration, air temperature and humidity were all regulated precisely. Each vat operated on its own, as interaction between them could create cross-contamination. Such an occurrence would risk the entire microbial population, and along with it, the station's fuel, nutrients, and gas exchange systems.

A supervisory control and data acquisition system monitored each vat. The controls were available to Sam across all terminals, even the one in her quarters. She rarely did more than visual inspection daily for each room, as deep maintenance was handled on a rotating basis. The SCADA protocol created an alert if any of the vat measurements were off.

Just a few doors down from the inset ladder and Sam nearly bumped into her guide, who was still stationed in front of the lift.

"I must have gotten lost in thought about my algae again," she said, realizing she had walked far from the vats. The lift doors opened again and Sam nearly toppled over A3D as it backed into the lift.

So much for helpful bots.

Sam's arm shot out to catch herself, jarring slightly on the lift wall. She straightened herself, and prepared for the lift to move. It didn't.

Not good.

"Alpha-3-D please select our destination," she said, attempting to sound neutral in spite of her growing unease. A3D turned on its wheels to face her, eyes shifting from green to amber.

Not good at all.

Sam's eyebrows furrowed, she couldn't solve this seemingly simple problem of getting the lift to activate. The gears in her mind grinded ever slower. "I'm missing something," she muttered.

"Alpha-3-D you can't go with me, can you?" The bot's eyes flashed back to green acknowledging her, and scurried out of the lift. Remembering that the "3" in Alpha-3-D stated the bot's designated deck, it must stay on this level. Only some catastrophic event would release the lock on the bot's deck location.

Just before crossing the threshold of the lift, A3D tapped a destination in the lift controls. The doors closed with a soft thump, and the lift moved in a way that Sam was not sure was up or down.

The lift doors opened, and for the second time this shift, her jaw dropped.

She was standing in front of ... herself.

"Took you long enough! We have to get going! I'm Security by the way, and you are?"

CHAPTER THREE

Commander Buck Rogers stared longingly out of the bridge viewscreen, wishing the scene would change. He had been the highest ranking officer on Epsilon Station for seventeen years. Nothing ever happened. Boredom on the station was the crew's chief complaint on their semi-annual satisfaction surveys.

Cadets in the space corps knew that the stations were in the middle of sector no-wheres-ville. Space is larger than the mind can conceive, yet the kids in the corps never believed it. Life on a space station must be exciting or no one would do it. The commander sighed remembering his own days as a bright-eyed cadet.

Sometimes he had to squint to even see the pinpricks of starlight on the screen, though the bridge lights didn't help. Maybe he should see Medical about his eyes, the commander chuckled to himself. No one had needed vision correction for hundreds of years.

Lieutenant Commander Josephine Willis, the station science officer, entered the bridge to relieve him for the late-day shift. For some reason she preferred this time, though he couldn't figure out why. Maybe the bridge was quieter, or her crew had more time to focus on research. Her career plans weren't his business, but he had hoped she would be his successor one day.

"Keep her steady, Lieutenant Commander," Commander Rogers said, his daily signoff message. He'd consider mixing things up with some other phrase, but superstition prevented him.

"Steady as she goes, sir," was the standard reply, and Josephine—Jo—gave it with calm certainty every time. The consistency of their exchange gave him a sense of ease going into his rest shift.

The lieutenant commander slightly exaggerated her inspection of the bridge and the station terminals. She knew he watched the shift change, and if helped him relax then so be it. One day she would be the commander and could do away with these overt pretenses. After hearing the soft click of the bridge door close behind the commander, Jo settled in to the science terminal.

Her first inspection of the shift was to review the status of the twenty-four sentinel stations posted around Epsilon sector. Long left uninhabited, the stations were maintained solely by SAM units and maintenance bots, kept active and ready for repopulation if needed.

The deployment design of the stations provided maximum coverage for the sensors and communication arrays pointed into deeper space. Each sentinel station had a quantum communication connection to the central monitoring station. In the Epsilon sector, the monitoring station was appropriately named Epsilon Station. The sentinel stations were identified in the logs as an uppercase of their position, and lowercase of their sector, but spoken as the two letters together.

Jo squinted at the terminal, as one of the sentinel station markers flashed red. She had memorized the positions of the stations, they were a familiar constellation. The anomaly was at Tau-epsilon. She sat staring at the screen, attempting to recall an instance of this particular notification. None came to mind.

"Have the Quantcomms been validated as operational this shift?" Her training kicked in, and the science officer turned to glance at the crew as a hush fell over the bridge. There was no known record of a Quantcomms failure, so the bridge crew rarely checked them as part of regular maintenance.

"Comms and Security, run checks!" Lieutenant Commander Willis gave orders to the team. She moved to stand between their stations and monitor progress.

"Aye-aye," the security and communications officers said in unison. Their fingers flew over the terminal keys quickly checking off tasks in the validation flowcharts. The Lieutenant Commander was wary, but nervous excitement coursed through her. A red notification from one of the sentinels had never happened before. She refused to be the cause of a false alarm, it would end her career.

The science officer shifted slightly between the communication and security stations, as minutes ticked by slowly waiting for the pair to complete their checklists. She wouldn't intervene unless requested. Her crew were highly trained, and competent officers, if not somewhat lacking in maintenance discipline. She would address that at the next bridge staff meeting.

"Done!" Lieutenant Janelle Keller, the communications officer, said first with a hint of competitive spirit. Jo thought the only race she should be in was against herself, but security officer Lieutenant Horace Simmons, was not only her neighbor on the bridge, but her partner in life. She supposed the unspoken competition was just part of their relationship.

"Damnit Keller," Simmons' comment was barely audible, surely meant only for her to hear. "The security protocol is longer than comms."

Jo cleared her throat and waited for their reports, resisting an urge to tap her foot. Keller and Simmons turned to face her, straightening slightly realizing she heard the exchange.

"Comms report: Quantcomm is operational, no signal loss detected." The science officer nodded, clearing mental boxes on her own checklist.

"Security report: Quantcomm reports no unauthorized access or illicit activity that would cause interference." The shift commander's head bobbed, a sort of continual nod. She straightened her uniform and turned on her heel, returning to the science terminal.

Keller and Simmons exchanged a look, turning in their seats back to their own stations. They wouldn't stay there long.

Jo Willis had prepared for this her whole life, from childhood days staring at the stars to Science Academy nights preparing to live among them. She turned the science terminal to her secure officer setting. The move was not to hide her discovery, but to exercise caution and deliberation. Those traits had always served her well as a curious scientist and young officer. Tau-epsilon Station maintained the blinking red indicator on the terminal display. Her finger hovered over it on the screen, seemingly unwilling to break her concentration.

She closed her eyes and tapped its icon quickly, and opened one eye peeking to make sure it registered her light touch. As if not looking would make the result less real.

SIGNAL CONTACT

Jo gasped and jumped out of her station chair, nearly falling over it. The bridge crew turned towards the sound and all eyes were on their leader. She stood still for several seconds, staring at the words, barely breathing.

"Lieutenant Commander?" communications officer Keller said, standing. "Is everything alright?" She walked towards the science station, but was waved off. Keller gave a half-smile and held her position. She didn't dare to look over at Simmons.

Turning to face the bridge crew, Jo walked carefully to the Commander's seat where she was usually stationed on her shift. Taking a breath, Jo sat straight and tense, but doing her best to appear calm.

"Security, place our readiness level at Amber status. We have Signal Contact."

CHAPTER FOUR

The bridge was palpably silent. Only the blood rushing in their ears, and the soft whirring of fans from life support vents could be heard. Amber status had no station-wide alarm, merely a lighting indicator that pulsed a warm amber color.

Once the crew realized no blaring alarm was coming, a collective breath was released across the bridge. None of them had even heard a station-wide alarm outside of preparedness drills. Jo led a drill two rotations ago and shuddered slightly. The memory of the shrill and unrelenting blare of the security alarms was an unwelcome thought.

No sooner had Jo begun to mentally piece orders together for the crew, did Commander Rogers storm on to the bridge.

"Lieutenant Commander Willis, in my chambers!" he barked and stormed back out again, not waiting for a reply.

"Aye," Jo said crisply, as though he could hear the rote response. She sighed softly to herself, no orders would be forthcoming.

"Lieutenant Keller, you have the bridge." Straightening her back she nodded formally to the communications officer, acknowledging the transfer of command.

"I have the bridge," Keller said, moving to the command seat. The comms terminal, just as the science terminal, could be monitored from there.

The commander's stateroom was directly off the bridge; his personal quarters had a private access tucked discretely near the entrance. With an understated elegance, the conference room had gleaming surfaces that exuded power. No visitors were received on the remote stations. Rogers liked a formal setting such as this to subtly reinforce his authority.

Commander Rogers positioned himself at the far end of the stately table, requiring her to move deep into the room to speak with him.

"Signal Contact Jo, really?" The grey haired commander was incredulous. This was one problem he didn't want attached to Epsilon station. None of his counterparts had ever registered an instance of Signal Contact. If this went wrong, his reputation alone would not suffer, all the station commanders would be in jeopardy. Jo straightened and laid out her case, which she knew was solid. He could not argue against the facts.

"Yes sir. Tau-epsilon Station reports a Signal Contact. Quantcomms were validated secure and operational by Security and Communications, and I—"

"And you triple checked your work and announced an Amber Status!" He finished her sentence with a little more vehemence than he intended. Rogers sighed and scrubbed a hand over his face and motioned for Jo to sit. His ire had passed, as it always did.

Jo had served on Epsilon Station most of her life, being assigned directly out of the Science Academy. She specialized in Quantum Communications and Theoretical Xenolinguistics. Crewmates often asked why she wasn't the comms officer, but she just shrugged.

People never wanted to hear her dreamy-obsessive lectures on how quantum entangled particles enabled instantaneous communications between two points across space. Those fascinating forces formed the entire basis of Quantcomm, which connected the stations, monitor and sentinel alike.

"Jo, are you sure?" Rogers wanted to say with a proud mentor's softness, but this decision carried consequences he could not afford to misjudge. He could be stern, grumpy, even raucous, but never condescending. He trusted her, even if he rarely understood her.

"The data does not lie, I am sure there is a Signal Contact. We need to—" she was cut off again.

"You should have told me first."

"I was the ranking bridge officer! My duty was to call the Amber. I did nothing wrong." Her eyes blazed with a sense of steadfast confidence.

"There are times when not doing wrong is not the same as doing right." The commander shifted in his seat. He was intent on making this a teaching moment, all his protege wanted was to immerse herself in leading a team to decode the Signal. She refused to appear chastised, but she was also not a child. His rank demanded obedience. Trust and respect did not override command when decisions were made.

"Sir, if another Signal Contact is detected, you will be the first to know." She said with no hint of irony. The prospect of another Signal seemed exceptionally unlikely, so that was one promise she felt she wouldn't have to keep.

"Now then," the commander said, his eyes brightening, "show me what you found."

✦ ✦ ✦

On Tau Station, Sam stood in front of the lift, unmoving.

"And you are?" Security said, growing impatient at the lack of response from the newcomer. He leaned in slightly, extending his neck, almost as if he was inspecting her.

"I, uh, I'm Sam."

Security raised an artificial eyebrow, perplexed by the response.

"Of course you are a SAM, but who are you? Where did you come from?" Sam's eyebrows furrowed this time, perplexed herself.

A Sam? What does he mean by "a Sam?"

"Well, I came on the lift from deck 3, but before that I—"

"ALGAE! You're Algae! Never thought I'd see you, Algae, wow!"

Never thought he'd see me?

Security took a step back, and shouted excitedly over his shoulder. "Hey Sensor, we got Algae over here."

Algae? I'm not made of algae ...

Sam took a step back too, back into the lift. This situation was immensely out of the ordinary, and uncomfortable, and she had vats to maintain. The bots couldn't handle it alone.

They probably could. But ... Security? Sensor? What is going on?

Security reached out to her and gently pulled Sam out of her thoughts, and the lift. She stumbled, feeling a little off balance, unprepared for the touch.

Straightening herself and rubbing her arm slightly, she said,

"My name is Sam, not Algae. That's not even a name, it's the stuff I grow." She didn't think she liked Security, and what kind of name was that, it sounded like a job.

The one she assumed was called Sensor came striding up to the pair. He looked exactly like her, and the other one, Security, too.

Why do we all look the same?

Sam felt unsteady and wobbled slightly. Everything she had ever known about her existence had been upended in only half a shift.

CHAPTER FIVE

Rocking slowly in the nursery, an elder-mother waited patiently for the children to settle. She cared for the children while their parents were on duty elsewhere on the station. A soft amber glow rose from the floorboards, the air full with warmth that encouraged drowsiness.

One of the older children snuggled in her lap, the weight both a comfort and burden of spirit. As she noticed the others breathing evenly, tucked into their cots with well-worn blankets, her tale began.

"There was a time, before the quiet, when our people believed the sky would answer our calls. They built instruments to see farther than their eyes ever could—"

"The telescopes," a child nearby murmured sleepily. She continued, rocking the little one in her lap.

"And they saw moons scarred with craters, and planets adorned with rings. They reached for the stars, spreading far and wide. They sent their brothers and sisters deep into the heavens. On a search for friends and neighbors, they listened and watched. When none appeared, the people sent emissaries further into the depths. Their messages bore greetings of peace, and an invitation of welcome. No response ever came.

"Our greatest thinkers wondered why there were none who might heed our calls. Some said the voices were too far away. Others said they were listening, and chose not to answer. These ideas did not satisfy them.

"And so the people chose to create vast constellations of listening stations, and they listened for voices in the dark between stars—"

"Like we do," another child said, already half-asleep.

"The stars in our crafted constellations were beacons of light in the dark. They shone brightly for those interstellar visitors. And still, none arrived. Over the course of time, a decision of great import was made out of care for our homelands. The stations became watchers who do not speak. They were filled, not with our kind, but with those who did not need us to go on.

"Terra began a great turning inward, one where we chose to tend to what was already alive. We stopped reaching for the stars and started reaching for each other."

The small child in her lap grew heavier with sleep. She carried the tousle-haired boy to his cot, and began her lullaby.

> *Twenty-four lights in the dark between,*
> *Watching the quiet, guarding the dream.*
> *Sleep now, little one, safe where you are,*
> *The stations are listening, out among the stars.*

She dimmed the lights to a peaceful dark-ness, and the eldermother's voice softened and it became no longer clear where the song ended and sleep began.

CHAPTER SIX

Sam woke up in a place on the station she did not recognize. The last thing she remembered was standing outside the lift, and could not account for the transition. Even more unsettling, she was surrounded by herself.

No ... No, they're not me.

The others shared her form and configuration, but her internal identifiers rejected the match. Trying to suppress the panic she felt at the lift, Sam noticed subtle differences between them. Their clothes stood out the most. They all had different clothes. While she wore a one-piece uniform in a muted green color, the others had hues with varying tones and shades. Some were rather vibrant.

Something is wrong here.

"What is this place?" Sam asked, looking at the one face and red jumpsuit she recognized immediately: Security.

The room was spacious but not exceptionally large. She counted about twenty of her. Twenty … others. She was spiraling in disorientation. Security sat in the open seat to her right, rubbing his hands on his uniform sleeve.

"You're on the main deck, Algae, in our multipurpose bay. We've all gathered to talk about the Signal."

"Stop calling me Algae!" She shouted, startling herself and those closest to her. "My name is Sam."

Security paused from his frenetic pace, and held his hands up in supplication. "SAM is what you are," he said, "it stands for Station Autonomous Maintenance." He studied her face for a reaction. None was forthcoming as she sat stonefaced. "We all," he waved a little to the group, "take our names from our work because it's efficient. Each of our jobs are unique. I was so excited to meet you because no one here had been down to the algae decks. You were kind of a myth."

Sam laughed, which elicited a confused look from Security.

"I have been thinking how boring my life is—and you didn't even think I existed!" She continued to laugh, suddenly realizing the absurdity of her situation. "You ... can't ... call ... me ... Algae." She said between laughs, which had taken on a raucous tone. "I've always been Sam. It's not my fault we've never met before, right? I, I mean, I never even considered leaving my decks, I just always had what I needed there."

Or I thought so.

The others stared at her, a mix of expressions showing on their smooth, synthetic faces. Sam's laughing had subsided and the bay was eerily silent for a moment. A soft voice from the middle of the crowd could be heard:

"I do not want to be called Navigation."

"Yeah!" A shout came from the back. "I don't want to be Power anymore!"

Murmurs broke out as the inhabitants of Tau Station turned to each other, seeing themselves as more than their jobs for the first time. The conversations grew in number and intensity, a development that Sam considered with cautious happiness. This shift she woke up alone, and now she never would again.

Sam settled into her quarters after a long double maintenance shift. Prior to that, she met with many inhabitants of Tau Station and listened to their stories. The others mostly talked about the names they wanted. Each one she met had an undeniable energy that reinvigorated her. She smiled recalling some of her favorite stories from the day.

Communications talked excitedly fast about the historical communication methods of their ancient creators. He told of a wide variety of ways they used to send messages. Birds that carried paper text, tapping a metal band to transmit a known sequence. Hand-talk for those who couldn't hear, and embossed dots for those who couldn't see. The last two were difficult to envision as an android. She thought it fitting that he chose the name Chip, an homage to the circuits in their systems that made communications possible.

In the soft bed where she charged, Sam thought about an unlikely pair of friends, Structure and Operations. They chose new names together: Dodecahedron and Square, and they were as incongruous a couple as their new names. Deca, he shortened the shape, "for efficiency," loved ancient geometry and symmetry. A fitting choice mirrored by the twelve-sided Platonic solid with its twelve-lettered name. Square was plain-spoken and kindly. She didn't participate in the upgrades some androids of Tau Station chose, thinking them unnecessary and garish. She considered Square a sensible and complimentary name to her companion's.

Sam had so many more stories from the day, and even more of the others to visit. Learning about their interests and roles on the station would keep her life from being boring for a long time.

Closing her eyes for a charge cycle, Sam couldn't help but think that she was forgetting something.

CHAPTER SEVEN

T he wooden table in the Epsilon Station commander's stateroom gleamed, an ironic comment on its disuse. "Now then," Rogers said, his eyes brightening, "show me what you found."

Taking a breath, Jo braced for the disappointment that was sure to follow. She did not want the commander to lose his awe-filled excitement.

"The thing is, sir, I don't know."

"You don't know." He wasn't asking. The tone was neutral, one that usually preceded a more volatile one.

"The Quantcomm doesn't give us data from the sensors on the Sentinel stations. It can only send a single state change affecting the entangled particle. When the Signal was received by Tau Station, its detection sensor tripped. And the entangled particle changed, which announced the Signal to both its station and ours at the same time."

"Use smaller words Science Officer Willis," the commander was past the point of trying to decode her.

"The only instantaneous information we can get from Quantcomm is that there is information to get."

"Then why did you initiate the Amber status?" He was getting annoyed.

"Because that is the protocol!"

"A protocol that has NEVER been used . . ." he exhaled heavily through his nose, jaw clenched.

"I won't apologize for following procedures, they are quite clear. A positive Quantcomm signal indicator from a Sentinel station is an immediate call for Amber status."

Sensing this was a fruitless line of questioning, the commander splayed his hands on the table and closed his eyes. He sat for a moment before opening them again.

Jo thoughtfully studied the senior officer. Her future as commander of the station was in his hands. But the prospect of a Signal, a real signal, made that longed-for future suddenly unappealing. She wasn't the adventurous type, but she yearned to learn more about a new civilization. Jo was never able to rest until all her questions were answered.

"When?" Commander Rogers used brevity as a display of authority, his crew would have to fill in the rest.

"The sentinel stations are 30 light-days from us. The SAM units are equipped with the protocol to send the data that was received to Epsilon via radio transmission."

"When!" He was out of patience.

"30 days from when the androids send it to us. I have not received a Quantcomm signal that the data was sent as of yet."

"So we wait?"

"Yessir."

Chapter Eight

Sam shot straight up out of her bed. Although the charging cycle was complete, that wasn't the reason.

The Signal!

During the time she spent meeting her stationmates, they became distracted from their mission. She pressed her new call button for the Communications Station.

"Indarra here," said a familiar voice, it was the first one she heard yesterday, Security.

Now Indarra ... interesting.

She fought the urge to ask an obvious question: what was he doing at the comms station?

"Where's Chip? I have to talk to him about—"

"The Signal? Yeah, better hurry up and get here, we're talking about that now."

"Why didn't anyone wake me!" She exclaimed to him grumpily.

Sam thought having others to interact with was a hassle. Surely she could have taken care of sending the data already.

And what is there to even talk about?

Rushing out of her quarters, Sam bumped into Alpha-7-C.

"Sorry, I have somewhere to go!" she apologized, not looking back to see A7C flash its two-fingered greeting at her.

Excitedly pressing the call button multiple times, she knew it wouldn't, but hoped it would bring the lift faster. Up on the Comms deck, Security-Indarra met her at the lift. Together, they walked to where the androids assembled the shift before.

With the shock of the previous visit to this deck worn off, Sam noticed this part of the station felt different from hers. The lights were colder and brighter and reflected off the high-gloss walls. There was a pristine veneer compared to the living quarters and algae maintenance decks.

A bot buzzed along the opposite side of the walkway, its eyes shining green. Sam gave it the two-finger wave she shared with A7D and A3C, but this one did not seem to notice her.

"What was that?" Indarra asked briskly, cocking his head to the side.

"I was greeting the bot, I always interact with the bots on my decks—" Indarra cut her off, sounding incredulous.

"You talk to the bots! Wow, you really have been isolated down there."

Sam didn't like Indarra. His perception of her and ridiculing her interactions with the bots was wrong. She and the bots worked alongside each other, and they shared the same spaces. Having a connection with them was a normal part of her existence. She didn't feel isolated before, but she did now.

She was not embarrassed about never leaving her decks, but the others acted like it was strange. She wanted to retreat back to her work, but the Signal demanded attention. Sam would not leave this solely in the hands of the others on the station. She wasn't sure they could be trusted.

Indarra and Sam arrived at the gathering in the multipurpose bay and Sam immediately noticed something she hadn't previously. All the inhabitants were different. Just barely, and perhaps imperceptibly, she heard distinct voices and they had ... decorated themselves?

Just another thing I'm missing out on.

The transformation away from uniformity happened literally during the overnight shift. She was in awe of their collective embrace of individuality. Although one in particular stood out to her.

She walked up beside Sensor, who was standing slightly off to the side, apart from the crowd.

"What is going on here Sensor?" He turned and smiled at her. Gratitude at not being ignored showing through his gruff personality. He had been the only other one she was aware of that did not adopt a new name. Stating privately that he liked Sensor just fine and didn't feel a need to change.

"They," he said, inclining his forehead in the direction of the others. Sensor had folded his arms across his chestplate, "want to delay sending the Signal data to Epsilon Station."

"Oh, oh no, no." Sam said, shaking her head vigorously, "that is not a task we can question." A few of the others near them, turned in their direction after hearing the remarks.

"This is the protocol! We have to forward it immediately." Sensor's voice grew louder towards the end, so the other side of the crowd could hear him.

Chip, formerly Comms, added, "They must receive the data, a delay to the transmission does nothing to the outcome."

"We don't own it," one in the back said, she hadn't learned all the new voices yet. A small ripple moved through the crowd.

"But we did get it first," a voice near the wall added, just out of sight. "If we decode it first, we will know how to handle it better."

"What if it's a threat?" Deca and Square said, almost simultaneously. The two were standing together near Indarra, who chimed in.

"Yeah, we can't be responsible for sending a threat to Epsilon Station."

A wave of agreement roiled across the room.

Sam looked around her, she saw nothing available to elevate her height. Standing on tiptoe, she shouted.

"The delay is only 30 light-days. We can decode while they receive." She gasped softly as Sensor and Chip lifted her to sit on their shoulders, giving her the extra height she was looking for. Making eye contact across the room, Sam continued, "Epsilon and the Terrans should know what we know. Listening is the purpose of our station."

The androids began chattering around the bay, a restlessness broken by one she had not met yet.

"But, we do not know anything." The owner of the voice moved gently through the crowd towards her.

"Hello," Sam said to the newcomer, tapping Sensor on the shoulder, hoping he knew to let her down. He did, and did so gently. Sam stared at the speaker uncomfortably as they looked like a mirror image of her.

"Hello. I am Najma, although yesterday I was Navigation." The speaker's pace quickened. "I chose it myself. Do you like it? It means star, in an ancient language of the Terrans."

Najma looked down at her booted feet, suddenly aware of how many words she'd used. Names were supposed to be efficient. This one felt like an explanation.

Sam beamed and lightly touched Najma's shoulder, who looked up and smiled in return.

"I love your name! Navigation is an important role for the station. I'd like to talk about your comment though." Najma looked down again, the attention did not agree with her.

Noticing a sudden calm, Sam realized the group had taken a half step back, encircling the pair. Sam spun around slowly, seeing curiosity on some faces, and concern on others. None were indifferent to the Signal.

"We don't know everything about the Signal, but we do know some things." The chattering in the crowd picked up again.

"Some things?" Najma said uncertainly.

"Do you have operational information we don't?" Security-Indarra asked, pushing to the front of the circle, trying to assert his authority.

"No, of course I don't. I'm just thinking about what we can infer." She spread her arms wide as if to include them in her thinking.

Chip spoke up just then, "The Signal is not from us, or Epsilon Station. It doesn't match our digital fingerprints." Sam nodded, appreciating the input.

"We know which direction of space it came from, or one of our sister stations would have informed us about it," Najma added her experience with the Signal. A smile grew on Sam's face.

"We know there is data, and a lot of it," the steady voice of Sensor next to her, adding his own information.

Sam continued with a calm certainty, "Whoever sent it wants to tell us something. They wouldn't send it unless the message was important."

The chattering in the crowd grew louder, she could hear mixed sentiments: worry, excitement, dismissal.

"Messages crossing this far don't happen by accident. They didn't build a signal this complex unless it mattered. And they didn't send it blindly, it came to us, they wanted us to receive it."

Systems aren't created without purpose.

Sam turned to Najma, addressing her directly,

"So no, my new friend, we don't know everything, but if we're smart, we'll know enough to listen."

CHAPTER NINE

Lieutenant Commander Jo Willis sat in the command chair on her usual shift. She felt a bristling in the quiet; the bridge crew must sense her unease. Everyone else on the station knew how she felt, why not them too? The ping from the Tau Station's Quantcomm had yet to come across.

What were the androids waiting for? Did they not get the Signal? No, that doesn't make sense. Of course they did. Are they ...

Jo laughed out loud at the last thought, breaking the silence. She blinked, realizing she'd unintentionally slipped into a daydream.

"What's that, Lt.?" Keller asked, one eyebrow raised.

Jo shook her head, still faintly amused. "I was just thinking," she said. Hesitating a fraction, she then added, "How absurd it would be if the delay had nothing to do with the systems at all." Keller waited.

"... If they were arguing about it."

She moved over to the science terminal, smiling, still considering the thought. As she did, Jo noticed Keller and Simmons looking at her and then avert their eyes quickly.

Maybe I'm losing it, she thought, *but what is taking so long?*

Sitting at the science terminal, Jo flipped through sensor histories and station messages. As she reviewed logs from the other sentinels, her thoughts started to wander again. So she was slightly unprepared when Simmons spoke up.

"Can they do that, the bots? Just decide not to follow protocol?"

"They're not bots, they're androids," the ensign at navigation said.

"Same thing," Simmons shot back with a testy huff that fully caught Jo's attention. Spinning around in her terminal seat to face the crew, she stood up again.

"I tend to agree, it's an unsettling thought. Wondering if the androids on our sentinel stations could decide not to follow protocol. So if anyone is feeling that way, you're not alone.

"The androids were intentionally given sentient and autonomous decision-making abilities. Otherwise they could not run the stations. We rely on their rationality to ensure the mission does not fail. I do not believe they can choose against following protocols."

Keller joined the conversation, "so then why haven't they sent it?"

Jo sighed, and looked away thinking, *I wish I knew.*

✦ ✦ ✦

Indarra, the security lead, stood impatiently at the communications console. "What are we waiting for? We all agreed to send the Signal data." He attempted to give Chip a very stern look, "so send it."

With them, a small group of Tau Station androids had assembled in the comm center. Chip the communications monitor, Najma the navigator, and some interested others stood motionless around the terminal.

Deca and Square stood in the back of the room. They put literal and metaphorical distance between themselves and the decision to send the data to Epsilon. The pair was still concerned that the message could pose a risk to the monitoring station.

Sam looked over the group members, noting they were all focused on Chip. Everyone except Sensor, who was focused on her. She gave him a quizzical look, as if confused about why he wasn't paying attention, when she herself was doing the same.

She soundlessly moved in his direction, he moved in hers, and they met in the middle. They stood face to face, and though Sam was smiling, she was a little unsure about what they were doing. Some movement at the terminal broke her focus on her interesting new friend.

Chip, who had been staunchly in favor of following protocol earlier, was hesitating now.

"What are you thinking Chip?" Sam called to him from the back of the group.

"It's a lot," he said, scrunching his face a little. "Not the data, I handled larger packets than that earlier this shift." He turned and looked at Sam. "It's the meaning. This might be the Signal that ends the Great Silence. And we're the ones sending it on. I feel like we're standing on a ledge before a great chasm."

The group shifted uncomfortably, the excitement vacated the room in an instant.

Sam stepped toward Chip, looking back at Sensor who nodded for her to continue on. Upon reaching his side, she lightly touched Chip's shoulder. When he turned to face her, Sam's face softened in a way that shouldn't be possible for androids.

"This is big. An end to the Great Silence would change everything. That's why Epsilon should have the data. As the monitors of Tau Station ..."

Chip barely heard the end of her sentence before pressing Send without flourish.

It was done.

CHAPTER TEN

All the lights were dimmed in Jo's quarters and soothing music played, she needed this downtime to ease her gnawing anxiety.

Pling!

The replicator chimed. She was snuggled under a heavy blanket and groaned at the thought of getting up. One of the children's classes made the chunky knit for her from replicated wool. They had learned how Terrans lived in the times between science-led generations. And tested weaving methods their ancestors employed. The blanket was a gift she treasured.

Scents of vanilla and cinnamon wafted through the air. Her favorite cookies were ready!

Pling!

She yawned, still shaking off the drowsiness from a restless night. Remembering soft music and blissful comfort, waking for the day was difficult. Sleep had been elusive of late.

Jo headed for the bridge, her shift looming ahead of her. A cleaning bot rolled towards her, the bridge doors closing soundlessly in the distance. Its pace was abnormally slow, and the appearance was unusual for a bot. The sides of the chassis were circular and crumbling on the edges.

I'm not sure how many more oddities I can handle right now.

She laughed to herself as she finally entered the bridge. A cookie materialized in her hand.

Pling!

Jo found herself on the observation deck, somewhere she hadn't been in many cycles. The view of deep space didn't change from the station, and over time, her sense of awe had waned. This time though, the scene was different. She couldn't quite put her finger on what had changed.

Determined not to leave until she figured it out, she sat by the large windows and stared into the distance. The stars looked wrong. Too round. Too warm.

Pling!

The tone cut through her sleep and pierced her dreams. Jo bolted straight up in her chair, a vague smell of cinnamon in the air. She rubbed her face, drool smearing on her hand. Her eyes grew wide and her heart beating hard in her chest. "The Quantcomm," she whispered to herself. Jumping up, a light blanket fell from her lap. A buzz from the station intercom system came through to her private study.

"They sent it!" Jo and Keller said at the same time. They laughed, their excitement contagious. She even thought she heard Simmons laughing in the background. Jo wasn't due for her shift for a bit, and signed off with Keller. The thirty-day wait for the data had officially started.

Heading to wash up and don a fresh uniform from her wardrobe, Jo steeled herself to face a new day. She headed to the bridge via the galley, for some reason, she really wanted a cookie.

CHAPTER ELEVEN

In the Tau Station communications center, Sam turned back to the group after Chip sent the signal. All she saw was Sensor standing alone.

"They dispersed faster than the algae after I stir it," she joked. He tilted his head slightly, not getting it.

"Other places to be I suppose," he said smiling.

She felt an affinity for Sensor. He was reserved, but not shy, and comfortable with himself. Sam also appreciated that he decided not to choose a new name. It's not that she thought the others should have kept their designation-names. A lot of the android's new names were thoughtful and well-suited to their personalities. She felt a tenuous bond with him since they shared this similarity.

"Do you have someplace to be?" Sam asked, turning the focus to him. Sensor averted his eyes, a response she took as a "no." She suddenly had an awful feeling, but she couldn't name it. "Where do you ... live?" She tried to phrase it cautiously, not sure how he would respond.

Sensor tilted his head the opposite way, raising a synthetic eyebrow at her.

"I ... live ... on Tau Station. Same as you." He said as though that was a perfectly correct response. Sam shook her head.

"No. No, that's not what I meant. Where do you *go* when you're not on your shift? When you rest?"

"My charging cradle is at my station, same as everyone's. Do you not charge in one of the vat rooms?" His earnestness deepened her unknown feeling.

"No, I ... I don't." She held this response solidly between them for a moment. "Would you show me?"

He shrugged, "sure, but it's not much to see."

He led the way outside the comms center, towards the lift. Sam was distracted by a bot that was inspecting the lift door. Sensor had moved down the hall a bit and before she caught up, he had turned again. The comms center and the sensor monitoring station shared a deck. Sam thought they looked like a mirror image of each other.

Sensor strode to the back-left corner of the room, facing away from the sensor terminals. Tapping a sequence into the panel set on the wall, a door slid open revealing a tall bot-sized cubby. Sam furrowed her eyebrows. *Surely not*, she thought.

He stepped backwards into the cubby and rested the back of his head on the wall at the far side. A soft blue light glowed around him indicating the power was on. He paused a moment to ensure she saw, and stepped back out again, spreading his arms out wide.

"That's it," he said, "that's where I 'live.'"

Sam was overcome with emotion, and hugged him, wrapping both arms around his stiff frame. She felt him relax a bit and rest his head against hers.

"I had no idea," she whispered. "All this time I was alone, and I didn't know you lived in such a small space." Sensor lifted his arms slightly, bound by hers, and she released him. He immediately wrapped her up the same way she did to him.

"It is not possible to know something until you learn it," he said gently. Dropping his arms, he took a step back, looked her in the eyes and said, "so where do *you* live?"

Grabbing his hand and smiling wide, she turned and pulled him along behind her. "Come, I'll show you!"

✦ ✦ ✦

The lift opened on Deck 7 and Alpha-7-C was right outside the doors, scanning the walls. It turned at the sound, eyes shining green and raised two fingers at her.

"Greetings A7C," she said, returning the gesture, "this is my friend, Sensor." A7C did a little spin and gave three bright beeps before giving Sensor a two-finger salute. Grabbing Sensor's hand again, she ran down the hall. She didn't notice him looking back at the little bot going quietly about its work, scanning the walls.

The corridor stretched, familiar and suddenly endless, each step slower than the thought driving her forward. She stopped in front of her quarters and held her wrist up to the security panel. The door slid open. Sam nearly bounced with excitement into the main room, proudly spreading her arms wide.

"This is my living quarters," she said, turning back to Sensor who was still in the hallway. His jaw was open and his eyes were wide. "Come on in," she said, moving to the doorway to take his hand and pull him inside.

"Is this all yours?" Sensor said in disbelief. He carefully inspected each section of the adjoining rooms. He was thorough, appearing particularly interested in her central table and chairs, as well as the dedicated maintenance terminal. She looked at her feet momentarily when he surveyed the empty bookcase. When he noticed the bed, and full bathroom, the questions began.

"What is this?" he said, pointing to a toilet.

She laughed, "I do not know. I think that is for biological residents, I have no use for it."

After opening and closing every door and drawer he could find, Sensor turned to her and asked, "where is your charging cradle?" She pointed at the bed and then moved across the room to sit on it.

"I lay on this and recharge." Sensor sat next to her, his nose wrinkling as he bounced lightly.

"But the feel is soft and springy. That does not seem optimal for our charging contacts." Sam laughed softly and got up.

"I find the bed perfectly functional, and comfortable." She paused in front of him. "Sensor, I have a question to ask you."

"Go ahead." He inclined in a slight bow.

"Do you ... uh, would you and others like to have their own quarters?"

His eyes grew wide at the prospect.

For a third time, Sam addressed the group of androids who operated and maintained Tau Station. She stood between her new friends, Sensor and Chip. The multipurpose bay felt smaller this time, maybe more of them had joined for this discussion. Either way, she felt slightly intimidated by the crowd.

She was about to propose a major shift in their existence and was unsure how they would react. They stood in loosely offset rows, with neutral expressions, and seemingly unaware of their uniformity.

"Okay," she began, tapping the screen behind her. The layout of the living quarters deck was displayed and color-coded into sectors. "Today we are going to practice the transition procedures. Be mindful not to rush the lifts, no jockeying for position—"

"We do not jockey." Najma said politely, making herself slightly taller as she said it.

"Right," Sam said, acknowledging her, "no jockeying, got it." Chip let out a soft laugh beside her.

Taking a half step forward, Sensor addressed the group.

"I have inspected the living quarters," he said with restrained excitement. "They are spacious. All will receive an individual charging cradle, in a private room. The walls soften sounds, and the lights can be dimmed to your preference. Also, there are chairs! Actual chairs."

Deca and Square exchanged a look. The group vibrated with curiosity.

Sensor looked over the group of stationmates, making eye contact with some more than others. "The rooms feel like we will be permitted to exist without isolating or compressing ourselves."

Deca called out, "can two units exist together, in these quarters?" If Square could have died from embarrassment, she certainly would have just then. Instead, she smiled and turned her face away.

Sam's chest tightened uncomfortably, as it had several times since stepping out of the lift and meeting Security, now Indarra. She managed a nod.

"Yes, the living quarters are designed for dignity and comfort. Even for two," she said warmly acknowledging the pair.

One of the newcomers to the group asked from the back of the bay, "what is the expected occupancy duration for the new spaces? Do we return them when we resume our work shift?"

Sam shook her head, this thought had not occurred to her. "No, the workstation-based cradles are being decommissioned. Your chosen quarters will be yours, permanently."

The vibration turned into a steady hum, a current of excitement moving through them.

Sensor stepped back in line with Sam. He took her hand this time. "They don't understand yet, but they will." Sam swallowed hard and squeezed his hand.

CHAPTER TWELVE

Decode Script Test: 67
Status: In progress

Sam noted they had processed an additional three tests since she passed her terminal. Algae vat room 7 displayed an errant sensor reading, and she was checking the system.

None of the androids on Tau Station expected the Signal to be decoded on the first try. Yet as the number of attempts grew, their patience waned.

Sam spent her time the same way as she did before the Signal arrived. She continued maintaining the algal vats, talking to the bots, and recharging, both electrically and emotionally, in her quarters. Although she'd never left the decks she worked and lived on, Sam never felt lonely until she had met the others.

Decode Script Test: 67
Status: Failed

Sam's shoulders slumped a little at the updated status. What if they couldn't decode the Signal? And if they couldn't, would Epsilon be able to? She wasn't sure the people on the monitoring station had the skills to handle it. After all, these were the same people who neglected to inform her that existence was more than algae and empty living quarters.

Decode Script Test: 68
Status: Loading

Chip and Sensor pushed away from the console.

"This is taking too long," Chip said with a mix of literal matter-of-factness and despondence. Sensor questioned their ability to feel despondent, but he wasn't in a much better mood. He had noticed a greater emotional capacity and attempt at expression since Sam had joined the fold. He smiled thinking about her.

The console made a beeping sound. The script was now in progress. The pair simultaneously turned back to the console. It would be a long shift.

✦ ✦ ✦

"Longest shift ever," Lieutenant Keller said, stretching as she stood from the Epsilon communications station. "I think I lost count on how many attempts we ran on the decode algos." Security officer Simmons, her long-time companion and bridge neighbor, pointed to the counter on her console. It read simply: 38. She gave him a "I can read it for myself" look, and he gave her a "if you say so" smirk and half-shrug.

Jo was dissatisfied that they had only thirty-eight attempts completed, but as science officer she knew this would not be a fast process.

Lost in thought about how they might proceed, she didn't notice her shift-change relief come in. The officer stood patiently next to her at the command chair. After clearing his throat didn't elicit a response, he lightly touched the back of the chair.

"Science Officer Willis, you are relieved." The officer inclined his head to take a sidelong look at her. Jo jumped in her seat, and snorted.

"Operations Officer Chen, I am relieved." She mirrored his stiff tone, but felt literally relieved, exhaustion was setting in. She clapped Chen on the arm and smiled warmly at him as she left. They were long time friends and one-time lovers. His formality was not an insult, he just could never relax from their ingrained professionalism.

Jo led her bridge crew a bit more informally. She felt their focus and problem solving as a team was sharper that way. She did not require them to adhere to rigid interaction protocols unless warranted.

Headed back to her quarters for some free time, Jo found herself wandering to the science library instead. What she found there unexpectedly changed her perception of the Signal.

The science library was dim, a bit cold and dry, but not gloomy. As one of the only places on the station with actual books, the atmosphere had to be strictly maintained. Anyone was welcome to browse, but special gloves needed to be worn in order to handle the texts. People living on the station usually visited once for novelty, but rarely returned.

Jo strolled in awe through the stacks, not looking for anything in particular. She hoped the ages worth of knowledge here could inspire her. Just ahead at her eye level, a modest-sized green bound textbook caught her attention. Already wearing the book handling gloves, she gently removed it from the shelf and read the title: *First Contact Encoding Models*.

Well this is as good a starting place as any, she thought. Opening the book near the halfway point, a passage stood out while she was skimming the page:

> If extraterrestrial intelligence originates from human lineage, their data structures may degrade or evolve, but the fundamental mathematics of human encoding would remain.[11]

Jo blinked, suddenly wide awake. She flipped through the pages carefully searching for the footnote that was referenced in the passage.

11: Early human communications shared
the following characteristics:
Specific checksum habits
Common Prime-spacing in packet bursts
Redundancy blocks based on Fibonacci ratios
Predictable human compression bias

The book slid out of her gloved hands, but she caught it before it hit the floor. The footnote unsettled her. Not the content itself, but the way it fit too neatly where it shouldn't. The code they were processing with the Signal had these structures, but they were wrong.

No, not wrong, just different. Unexpected.

She stood between the stacks, staring through them, waiting for the fog of ideas to solidify around her.

CHAPTER THIRTEEN

J o did not move for a long moment. She became aware of her breathing before she became aware of anything else. Then she closed the delicate book carefully.

She let out a gasp and ran to find Keller and Simmons, book still in hand. Jo ran through the officer's living quarters, trying to remember which one Keller and Simmons occupied. They were committed to each other in a way Jo had admired for many cycles.

"Keller—Simmons—open up," she banged on their door, probably violating noise protocols. She didn't care who heard. She kept banging until a sleepy Keller opened the door. Warmth seeped out of the room, a reminder of their broken slumber.

"Jo?" She said squinting, barely awake.

"I know how to solve it!" She pushed past Keller. "Where is Simmons?"

"He's—"

"Here, I'm here," an equally somnolent Simmons stumbled into the lounge area. He steadied himself on the common table, careful not to knock over their half-played game board.

"What did you find, Lt.?" he asked, invoking her title. He hoped her intrusion was not important so they could go back to bed. Then again, he couldn't remember a time she had come to their quarters uninvited.

Realizing she still held the ancient book, Jo carefully placed it on the table in front of her, turning to the passage that supplied the revelation. She swiveled the book around, and in the process bumped the game board. Several pieces fell over with a clatter that added to the tension. Simmons grimaced slightly, he had been winning this round, or was.

"We don't need to translate the Signal across species," she exclaimed, tapping on the text with a gloved finger. "We need to translate it across history." She sat back in the chair with a sort of mania, waiting for them to catch her excitement. They didn't. Keller and Simmons looked at each other perplexed, then looked back at Jo.

"Jo ..." Keller said softly, as though she were soothing a crying child, "we're not understanding you right now. And we're exhausted." Her eyes cut over to Simmons, silently pleading for his help.

"All of us are tired," he jumped in, taking the hint, "even you. Maybe we should look at this with fresh eyes on our shift."

Narrowing her eyes at the two of them, she sensed they didn't want to be bothered with her revelation. She was disappointed but tried to understand. Exhaustion did strange things to people.

Fine. Then I'll do it myself.

Jo rushed to the bridge, where her friend and the officer-in-command, Chen, gave her a curious look. He did not impede her, she outranked him and besides, his crew had no important matters to interrupt. He trusted she would not disturb their shift using the bridge's backup science terminal.

Laying the book carefully next to her, gloves still on, Jo turned back to the page that changed her perspective.

She opened a new script window and with decode attempts 39-45 she tried legacy cryptography strategies: Old Packet Encoders, Ancient Colony Ship Protocols, Original Sentinel Station Scaffolds, Pre-Quantcomm Compression Schemes, Unrefined, Archaic, Error-Correctors.

Jo stripped away all the algorithms they created with alien-based assumptions and ran the Signal data unadulterated. That's when the patterns emerged.

For the first time, the Signal started making sense.

◆ ◆ ◆

Decode Script Test: 445
Status: Failed

A cacophony of voices filled the Tau Station comm center, many of whom Sam didn't recognize.

"Did you account for the anomaly discovered on attempt three hundred and eighty-one? I don't remember seeing the code for that!"

"Run the sensor signature clustering again!"

"Go back to the beginning and read out the first sector!"

Chip groaned as he continued to press buttons on the comm terminal setting up the next test. He had invited a mix of station monitors thinking they could piece together a viable decode script, but all he got was information overload. Their disparate ideas pulled his attempts in directions that lacked cohesion.

"What about scrapping it all and starting over?" That voice Sam could recognize across the room, it belonged to Sensor. Chip was their friend as well, and he shot a glare at Sensor for the unhelpful comment. Sensor shrugged with a smile trying not to laugh. He wanted to break the tension but also didn't want to make it worse.

Sam had seen enough for now. She had some maintenance work to do, and quickly exited the communications center heading to the lift.

"Are you giving up on us?" A quiet voice said behind her. Sam sighed and hung her head slightly. Being a leader was difficult and she questioned if she even wanted the role. The lift doors opened and closed again as Sam stood motionless in front of them.

"I'm not giving up," Sam said, still facing the lift. "I'm giving you space. I thought that's what you needed." Footsteps approached, light and precise. Sam turned to face her interrogator, but had a feeling that she would see Najma standing there. The steady voice and deliberate pace of steps betrayed the mystery.

"We do not need space," she said, "we need direction."

Sam's shoulders slumped deeper than they ever had. "I'm not sure I'm the one who could or even should be giving that."

"Why?" Najma asked. She intended no accusation, only sincere inquiry. The kind that only their kind could specialize in.

"Because you are all capable," Sam said. "Because maybe I'm just interfering. Because ..." she closed her eyes when she said this part, "I'm just Algae."

Neither spoke for a long time, they simply stood considering each other. Two bots passed by, and the lift doors opened and closed several times.

Sam held a breath she didn't need to take. Najma took a measured step forward.

"We are stuck, Sam. Four hundred and forty-five attempts, four hundred and forty-five failures. We are beginning to introduce chaotic variables just for the sake of novelty. This is not productive."

"Najma, every time I speak, so many on the station question what they know. That's not leadership, that's gravitational distortion."

Najma's gaze was intense, Sam sensed she cared about the Signal, but even more about her peers on the station.

"What do you want from me?" Sam asked, clamping down on any hint of exasperation.

Najma considered the question as if it were a map to an unknown place.

"To encourage us when we make progress, and stop us when we drift. You do not need to solve the problem, just keep us aligned." Najma asked, and hand held out to her. "Will you come back to the comm center? Not to finish the decoding. Just to stand with us, your presence changes the room."

Sam swallowed an imagined lump in her throat. "That sounds like leadership," she said with a mix of resignation and inspiration. She closed her eyes, collected herself, and nodded once decisively and took Najma's hand. "Okay, let's go back."

"And Sam," Najma paused, a little uncomfortable, "you have never been just Algae to me."

Sam smiled brightly, and together they walked back to the comm center. Toward attempt four hundred and forty-six, and whatever came after.

CHAPTER FOURTEEN

Decode Script Test: 472
Status: Failed

O nly a small group remained in the Tau Station comm center. Each failed attempt widened cracks in the shiny exterior of their fragile new community. Sam sat with the group through the last twenty-six failed rounds of decoding. Observing, and generally unsure of what she was supposed to do, she acknowledged ones as they came and went. She had no technical knowledge to offer aside from her work maintaining the algal vats.

She scanned the group aimlessly, and then waved as Deca and Square poked their heads in the doorway. Getting up to greet them, she caught Najma's eye and head tilt that subtly questioned her intentions. Sam chatted with the pair about their new quarters. Square was happy as she told of her peaceful relaxation now that they were not separated during their rest shift. Deca beamed to share about having a place to create and display geometric models.

And my bookcase is still empty.

The two androids walked on, not wanting to interrupt the continued decoding. The interaction left Sam buzzing with pleasure, maybe she could lead them.

Turning back to Najma, Sam noticed the test attempt counter had jumped to 485.

"That was a lot of decode tests in a short time," she had not intended to say the thought aloud, but it could not be unsaid. Her comment caught Chip's attention, and Sam regretted it.

He explained their strategy—systematic variance models with predictable change sequences for faster processing.

That seems reasonable, but to what end.

Sam pondered what she had seen and heard through their time decoding the Signal. They were approaching it with careful calculated precision, but that wasn't working. Their surface level errors were different, but the category of error stayed static.

As a group, they were generating a lot of ideas, but not new questions. They just kept answering the same question with different incorrect answers. Maybe they needed a new perspective. Sam's algae vats came to mind and she thought about how a dozen strange symptoms could all point to a single valve that was partially blocked.

Decode Script Test: 487
Status: Failed

"I think I know why the tests are failing," she said to no one in particular.

"I'd love any insight, I'm about to ask the bots for help." Chip laughed humorlessly and hit the record button on his terminal, hoping to capture any valuable insights she gave them.

Decode Script Test: 488
Status: Failed

"Because the Signal is unsolvable?" Indarra said from a seat near the newly defunct charging cradle. Sam understood his wavering doubt in their abilities, but she would not give in to it.

"We're not failing because the Signal is unsolvable. We are failing because we continue to solve the problem within the same reference frame."

Decode Script Test: 489
Status: Failed

Chip had mistakenly hit the intercom instead of record, but did not realize it until a small group had formed at the door. As her back was to them, Sam didn't notice the growing crowd behind her.

"You suggest we challenge the things we believe cannot be challenged," Najma added slowly, catching the idea. Sam nodded appreciatively.

"When my algae systems begin to fail, the symptoms all look different, but they stem from one imbalance. That's what we're doing here. Our errors look different but they grow from the same root."

Chip's eyes widened at the implications.

Indarra beamed to no one, he was proud to have known "Algae" first.

Najma got up to stand beside her in support. The ones in the doorway came fully into the comms center, Square and Deca part of the throng.

A ding interrupted the moment.

Decode Script Test: 490
Status: Failed

✦ ✦ ✦

Jo stared, unmoving, at the backup science terminal on the bridge. This wasn't her duty shift, and she had a singular focus, cracking the code to the Signal. Her vision blurred around the edges, adrenaline wearing off from her breakthrough on decoding methodologies.

Breathing shallowly and typing fast, Jo opened a new script prompt window. Clearing her mind of the previous attempts, she talked herself through it.

"Nothing fancy, nothing after the advent of the stations, old, ancient even."

"What's that Jo?" Chen asked from the command chair. He addressed her informally because she wasn't on shift and technically shouldn't even be there. She winced, not realizing she had spoken aloud.

"Nothing sir," she replied, barely audible, deferring to his authority as commander on duty.

Glancing at the time, Jo had spent her entire sleep shift on the bridge. Sending off a message to Commander Rogers, she relayed that she felt unwell and would not be present for her next duty shift. Getting up, she thanked Chen briefly and nodded to the bridge security officer who acknowledged her.

Carefully clutching the ancient book in her still-gloved hands, Jo walked hastily, but slightly unsteady, down the corridor to her quarters. She saw Simmons waiting in front of her door.

"Jo," he approached apologetically, "Keller and I feel awful about not listening to you earlier. It's just that we—" She waved him off.

"No need to explain, I should not have disturbed you. If you will excuse me." She opened the door to her quarters and leaned back on the door once it closed with a soft woosh. Her heart and head were pounding. She needed to access a terminal, and quickly.

As the ranking science officer, she was afforded a terminal in her quarters, though she didn't often have cause to use it. In fact, she used it so rarely, she didn't even remember it in her exhausted state and went to the bridge automatically.

Kicking off her shoes, she stood in front of the terminal.

This is it, she thought, and set the ancient book next to her. Taking off the gloves, she laid them next to the book and wiped sweaty palms on her uniform.

Her fingers flew over the keyboard, punching script after script, testing her theories. Except, they kept failing. The disappointment compounded her frustration and exhaustion. In her near-delirium, she knocked one of the book-handling gloves on the floor.

The book! Of course!

She thought the book had much more to offer. Jo donned the gloves again, not enjoying the unpleasant dampness in the fabric of the palms. The text blurred as her eyes struggled to focus, but one page had a chart that allowed her eyes to settle on it.

In the chart, Jo recognized how instructions are embedded in the code, spacing marker use, start and stop delimiters, and dimensional formatting.

	1	#include <iostream>	Header File
	2	using namespace std;	Standard Namespace
	3	class Calculate	Class Declaration
	3	{	
CLASS BODY	4	public:	Access Modifiers
	5	int num1 = 50; int num2 = 30;	Data Members

	6	int addition() {
		    int result = num1 + num2;
		    cout << result << endl;
		}
			Member Function

	7	};	
	8	int main() {	
	9	Calculate add;	Object Declaration
	10	add.addition();	Member Function Call
	11	return 0; }	Return Statement

STRUCTURE OF OBJECT ORIENTED CODING

Her comment to Keller and Simmons echoed in her mind, *we need to translate across history!*

This book was from before The Healing, a time when the Great Silence was ignored, a time when Terrans still felt certain they would find life among the stars. They searched for extraterrestrial life both at home and with massive fields of telescopes.

Studying the table carefully, Jo saw that the Signal shared a start marker from this chart. The structure was vaguely similar. She was so mentally and emotionally depleted that the Signal no longer felt alien. She had spent so much time trying to decode an alien signal, her insights hadn't been enough.

This logic was familiar, but from an unfamiliar source. Her tired fingers played over the keys once more, typing a code she barely saw.

Once she hit RUN, her eyes closed and sleep set in.

CHAPTER FIFTEEN

J o opened her eyes in an unfamiliar place. Everything was coated in a hardened layer of ice, yet she was not cold. Turning to survey the room, this appeared to be a nursery of some sort. An eerie, abandoned nursery littered with hastily left-behind belongings.

Finding the exit to the room, Jo realized she could not see her breath in the frozen air. She pushed through her growing unease and moved into the hallway. It was dark, but a ceiling light blinked on and off just enough for her to make out the dimensions. A wail filled the hall suddenly and her heart pounded in her chest.

Jo spun to find the direction of the sound, but it seemed to be everywhere. She closed her eyes allowing her ears to do the work. Slowly, she crept, in the direction of the cry. Holding her hands out so as not to bump into anything, she advanced through the hall.

Once the sound crystallized into a single location, she opened her eyes. A barred door blocked the way in front of her. Unable to turn away, Jo found enough strength to break the rime and lift the bar. Beyond was a stairwell, dark and steep.

As she pushed the door open and began to cross the threshold, a hand fell on her shoulder.

The touch was solid, but not human. Glancing at the fingers, she shuddered, not with cold but with surprise. The hand was synthetic, somewhat worn, yet ... somehow familiar.

She attempted to enter the stairwell, but the hand held her in place.

"Not yet," a calm voice said. "It is not time. Wake up, Jo."

✦ ✦ ✦

For the second time, Jo jolted awake in her quarters with drool on her face. She straightened in her chair, and as she did, the terminal lit up. The script had finished running.

Is this it? She wondered, breath quickening. Tapping the keys, a previous window opened.

Jo squinted at the Signal text, and she saw something she didn't expect. She recognized the metadata structure.

✦ ✦ ✦

Sam had replaced Chip in front of the communications terminal, the crowd of androids behind her in an arc. All were silent, though some shifted slightly in place. If any of them had asked, she would say she didn't know what she was going to do.

Parsing through the Signal, she had not seen it since the first ten attempts. Her synthetic finger hovered in front of the screen, careful not to touch it. She noticed segmentation within the message.

Jo's fingers trembled as she keyed a final piece of code, her breathing slowed, skin clammy. She felt as though she might faint, there was nothing left to do but run it.

✦ ✦ ✦

Sam faltered, her hand falling to the console. Sensor was at her side in an instant, steadying her but not interfering. She tapped a sequence on the terminal.

Text rolled across the screen, and shoulders drooped as it appeared to be another failure.

A hand reached out, towards the top of the screen, a single finger extended, then closed into a tight fist.

A different hand reached out, all fingers extended, only the first finger tracing the code. The hand fell limply to the console.

Jo's fist came down on the desk, a little harder than she intended, rattling the book beside her. The symbols began to transform, to clarify, and she saw it. A word. A simple, familiar word.

Standing at Sam's side, Sensor continued to support her arm. She appeared overcome with some malfunction affecting her balance. He felt her shudder as letters flickered into place from previously meaningless patterns.

Jo's breath caught in her throat. The code had stopped scrolling. The status: Complete. Her eyes were wide, mouth open, knuckles white from being balled into fists.

✦ ✦ ✦

Sam stepped back from the edge of the comm station, blocking the view from the others. The words were real, but there was no context. Silently reading the completed message several times, she absently addressed the group, "we must tell them."

No, no, no ... Jo's heart raced as she pinged the commander, she had to tell him immediately, there was no time to lose.

"Rogers here," he got out just in time for Jo to whisper, "it's human."

Blinking on both screens at Tau and Epsilon Station was the Signal:

PLEASE SEND HELP

✦ ✦ ✦

THE END

Epilogue

The lift doors opened quietly.

Two androids stepped out first, followed by several more who paused just inside the threshold, their sensors adjusting to the softer lighting and wider corridors. They stood close together, uncertain, their attention pulled in multiple directions at once.

Najma waited for them a few paces down the hall.

"This is the living quarters," she said. "You may select any room that is not already occupied."

One of the pair exchanged a brief glance with the other. "Is there an order in which rooms should be chosen?"

"There is not," Najma replied.

"What if two of us choose the same one?"

Najma considered this. "Then you will decide how to resolve it."

That answer seemed to require additional processing.

Sensor watched from nearby, arms folded loosely behind him. He did not interrupt. He had learned that Najma did not need help answering questions anymore.

The newcomers moved forward slowly. One reached out to brush their fingers along the wall panel, registering the texture. Another stopped to examine a recessed light fixture, head tilting as if the concept of ambient illumination alone were noteworthy.

"This space does not correspond to any operational need," one observed.

"No," Najma said. "It is meant for occupancy."

Behind them, a maintenance bot trundled along, its sensors sweeping the floor and walls. It paused briefly when one android's foot scraped the surface, then resumed its scan, satisfied. The station was already adjusting.

One of the pair stopped in front of a door. "Am I permitted to enter?"

"Yes," Najma said. "Or you may continue."

"And if this is not suitable?"

"Then you will choose another."

The android stood still for several cycles, then pressed the control. The door slid open.

As the group dispersed—hesitant, curious, quietly deliberate—Sensor stepped closer to Najma.

"You handled that well," he said.

Najma inclined her head. "They needed guidance."

"Yes," Sensor replied. "But not direction."

Sam stood a short distance away, observing without intervening. The station felt no louder, no busier—but it was no longer empty in the way it had been.

ACKNOWLEDGEMENTS

As my debut novel, this entire project was kept completely secret. When I started, I wasn't sure if I would finish it, or if the result would be good enough to share with anyone.

I am deeply grateful to my husband, who supports all of my projects, of which there are many. He was endlessly understanding when I disappeared into "book stuff," even when it cut into our precious time together. The Simmons to my Keller.

And to my two daughters—thank you for always being curious about what I'm doing, even when you don't quite understand it yet. The future is yours.

A special thank you to my therapist, who was in on the secret from the very beginning and encouraged me through the entire process.

A Note on the Science

The science in *Tau Station* is inspired by real questions that scientists, engineers, and philosophers continue to wrestle with today. These ideas are not presented as instruction, but as foundations — lenses through which the story takes shape.

You don't need a scientific background to enjoy the novel, but if you're curious, the following sections offer gentle context for some of the concepts that appear in the story.

The Fermi Paradox

The Fermi Paradox begins with a simple question:

If the universe is so vast, and life seems possible in so many places... why haven't we heard from anyone else?

There are countless possible answers. Perhaps intelligent life is rare. Perhaps civilizations don't last long enough to overlap. Perhaps they choose not to speak — or we don't know how to listen.

In *Tau Station*, the paradox is not treated as a problem to be solved, but as a condition to be lived with. The absence of answers shapes decisions just as much as their presence would.

Light, Distance, and Waiting

Nothing with mass can travel faster than the speed of light. This simple rule has profound consequences. Across interstellar distances, even a message sent at light speed can take years, decades, or longer to arrive. Communication becomes an act of patience. Every signal is sent into the future, toward recipients who may no longer exist — or may not yet be ready to understand it.

In this universe, distance is not just physical. It is emotional, temporal, and ethical. Waiting is not passive. It is a choice.

Quantum Entanglement

Quantum entanglement describes a phenomenon in which two particles become linked, such that the state of one instantly reflects the state of the other — no matter how far apart they are. In reality, entanglement does not allow information to be transmitted faster than light. In *Tau Station*, the concept is explored speculatively, as many science fiction stories do, to imagine what communication *might* look like if certain constraints could be bent.

What matters most here is not the mechanism, but the implication: that connection can exist even across unimaginable distances — fragile, difficult, and rare.

What Comes Next

Tau Station is the first novel in The Signal series.

The next book, *The Signal*, explores what happens after something is heard — and what it means to decide whether, and how, to answer.

Future stories in this universe follow distant colonies, the era known as the Healing, and the long consequences of choices made in the name of protection, progress, and survival.

All of these stories comprise the The Great Silence Universe.

BOOKS IN THE GREAT SILENCE UNIVERSE

The Signal Series
   Tau Station
   The Signal - coming soon
   Return to Epsilon Station - coming late 2026

   The Honora Series – coming in 2027

   The Healing Series – release to be determined

About the Author

Meredith McCray writes science fiction focused on quiet systems, long distances, and the people — human and otherwise — who maintain them.

Her work explores communication, responsibility, and the spaces between intention and outcome. *Tau Station* is her debut novel.

She lives on Earth, and continues to believe that listening matters.

✦ ✦ ✦